In loving memory of the world's
smallest, most efficient Esoteric
Studies Department:
Cambridge, MA, 2008-2010.

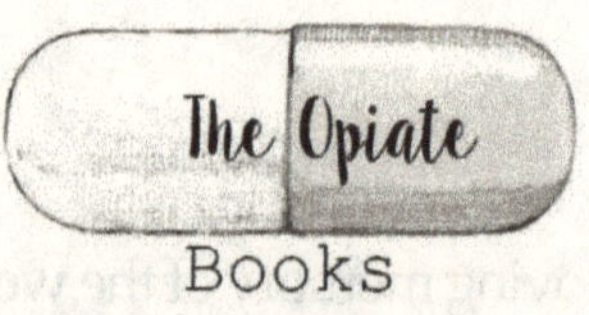
The Opiate
Books

"MY REACTION TO PORNO FILMS IS AS FOLLOWS: AFTER THE FIRST TEN MINUTES, I WANT TO GO HOME AND SCREW. AFTER THE FIRST TWENTY MINUTES, I NEVER WANT TO SCREW AGAIN AS LONG AS I LIVE."

-ERICA JONG

TABLE OF CONTENTS

FOREWORD

Prescience is not a quality every writer can lay claim to. Yet at the core of David Leo Rice's vast breadth of work has always been this characteristic. This includes his first piece for *The Opiate* back in 2015, entitled "Joey in Vermont." It was another narrative with a predilection toward highlighting disembodiment from one's corporeal self.

Playing into the no-longer-so-futuristic themes of being controlled by a screen (and the pornography on it), as well as a sort of lack of identity tied to that aspect of the self becoming an extension of a droning machine, *The PornME Trinity* is part hyper-real in its surrealness and part undercutting damnation of how the increasingly corporate-in-its-profiteering-schemes porn industry (and all tentacles thereof) manipulates its users. Preys upon them with the constant brainwashing tease of: "Oh but for just x amount more money, you could see *a much* higher tier of sordid perversity."

This is the sort of "getting them on the hook" economics behind the folks at PornME trapping our antihero (before he becomes just another hopeless sap in total non-control of his destiny, like the rest of us) into an eternity of being forced to enjoy "the perks" of his subscription. One can easily envision the likes of Amazon Prime, Netflix, Hulu, et al. taking this forcible approach to ensuring a forever customer not just in life, but in the so-called afterlife, to boot (though, sadly, there seems to be little difference between floating in the ether of space as one drools mindlessly over porn scenarios and sitting in an office doing pretty much the same within the confines of one's "work" station).

As Gribby becomes an ever-evolving cautionary tale against the purported temptations of the two-dimensional flesh, we, the readers (gobbling up our own form of porn), can't help but experience a similar detachment, an ironic form of empathy, if you will. Yet it harkens back to that aforementioned quality of Rice's writing: prescience. No longer is this notion of "empathetic detachment" an "unbankable" genre, so much as the new normal of the twenty-first century and its literature. And The Opiate Books is proud to publish one of its trailblazers in the arena of reflecting this strange era, wherein seemingly everything and nothing is available to us.

To quote one of Rice's characters, "It doesn't feel shocking to still exist, though it's no relief, either."

Genna Rivieccio
January 2020

POST-SCRIPT ON PUBLISHING A SECOND EDITION

Maybe the world wasn't fully "ready" for Gribby in early 2020, a.k.a. the months leading up to The Pandemic. Then, in March, when all the U.S. (or at least the select sect of it comprised of office workers who were not based in red states) would be forced into an even bleaker version of Gribby's existence as they took to their screens and surrendered to "just watching" and "enjoying," it was as though Rice's character had touched all-too-eerily on a long-flatulating zeitgeist. That unavoidable "new normal" was part of it, complete with a day spent almost entirely on Zoom, where it was suddenly never more obvious that the requisite eight hours of "working" (read: pretending to work) is completely absurd and superfluous. A unique breed of cruel and unusual punishment.

Of course, not everyone was "lucky" enough to be able to see themselves in different sexual scenarios with their co-workers by watching deep-fake porn like Gribby, but they were definitely more attuned to this "protagonist's" only-too-common form of an atrophying "life," wherein the screen becomes an extension of the self—and, maybe, even more of a "self" than the actual person planted in front of said screen.

Gribby is what Rice has retroactively classified as the "heroic pervert." By Rice's definition, this is "a character who becomes heroic not by venturing out to slay the dragon and save the village, but by willingly and knowingly succumbing to the sickness and depravity of a given moment." That "moment" is this post-Trumpian, post-COVID climate in which no one is really sure what "the social contract" is anymore, nor do they much care. For who among us hasn't been unapologetically guilty of such devil-may-care behavior in the days and years since the rona came to roost? Because what does flying your freak flag at full mast matter when presented with the ubiquitous threat of imminent death? If not by this virus, then surely by the next one conjured by climate change-related phenomena.

And this is where Gribby is also onto the wave of "the future" (happening as we speak): no one of the current generation seems to be even remotely as interested in tactile sex as they might have been in the pre-pandemic past. It's just too damn anxiety-inducing. Plus, with "services" like PornME, there's no risk of subjecting oneself to disease… unless you count the various diseases of the mind that have run rampant ever since porn's first major debut on the internet, however unofficial: the sex tape of Pam and Tommy. Whose "shenanigans" look positively puritan compared to what Gribby (and the rest of us) is watching.

Genna Rivieccio
September 2022

SON

Life in the surveillance state sure has its perks, as Gribby will be the first to tell you. Like this morning, for instance, as he's drinking his Ovaltine and Googling "guppies"— he has a tankful in the living room that won't quit dying—he comes across an email in his spam folder from a site called PornME that sounds interesting, so he clicks it open and it is.

It says, "We're watching ya all the time anyway, at work and home and everywhere and stuff, so why not pay a lil' extra to have yr vids porned up, bubba xoxo?" Gribby's intrigued. He likes porn as much as the next chump, and more especially, he figures, the kind made of vids of him and his co-workers—there's this gal Kellyanne he's always been kinda into, for one thing—so, *what the hell*, he figures, *sure, why not pay $12.99/ mo. and see if they can really, as they claim*, "Send ya one sexy vid per weekday featuring you and whoever ya been caught on camera with, rendered so realistically y'll swear you were there, which, come to think of it, haha, ya kinda were bubba ya know what I mean? Xoxo!"

Gribby inputs his credit card and waits open-mouthed for confirmation to arrive. Then he washes his hands, though they're not exactly dirty, and spills out the Ovaltine he forgot to drink and flushes his dead guppies down the toilet and chucks the tank to the curb after he walks out the door of the apartment he lives in alone except for a parrot named Graham—his own real name, from back before kids started calling him Gribby in the seventh grade, a slight step up from Goblin, which they'd called him before that, back when he was chubby—and up the street, down to the subway, and back up to another part of the same street and along it to the office he works in with a bunch of ugly and a few sexy people like, as he probably already mentioned, Kellyanne and Mr. Veitch, his boss, a pretty toned and tan older dickhead Gribby can't help but admire.

He walks into the weird smelly office and plops down at his particleboard desk and says, to no one in particular, "Here goes nothin'," and proceeds, like he just said, to do nothing at all.

He sits there all day, filing files, whispering into the phone when it rings filthy with yahoos, wondering the whole time when and from where he's being filmed, and what the gnomes or Pakistanis or whoever they are at PornME are doing with the footage, how they're hopefully already porning it up so when he gets home and cracks open his inbox what should be waiting for him but a brand new sexy vid starring his own self?

He can't believe it. Even though he knew it'd be there because he paid $12.99 and they promised, still, when he opens the file and actually sits back and watches himself humping Kellyanne on a stack of papers like a wild boar in the Maytime, he's pretty much stunned. He can just barely remember the moment when he passed her desk—it was right after lunch, pea soup on his shirt pocket, mayo or sour cream on hers, and he leaned in and said, kinda sexy-like, "Hey, mind if I use the copier?" And she shrugged without looking up and said, "Nah."

He remembers it now, however vaguely, but the memory's dying under the furious noise and sweat of the vid. He's plowing her like mad now, her skirt up around her waist, his pants down around his ankles, his ass grey with office dust, everyone else typing at their stations like everything's normal, which, as far as they can tell, it is. The PornME folks have done an ace editing job— everything looks real as can be, so much so that Gribby can't help looking at the version of himself in the vid and thinking, *Hell yeah, that's right, that's me up there, bubba!*

He cums behind his computer just as he also cums onscreen, on Kellyanne's slightly chubby belly—she's by no means as hot as the gals he might watch in any number of free porn vids online, but she's his, there onscreen with him and not some other dude he doesn't even know.

Wiping himself off before zipping the dick window of his full-body foot pajamas, he wonders, not quite knowing how this whole thing works, if it's possible to cum at two different times, or if that'd be like being in two places at once. He shrugs and orders dumplings from the Chinese place down the street and makes a martini with the last olive from the jar in the back of the fridge, then sits on his couch to wait.

This goes on all week, each day's vid sexier than the last—he's pounding Kellyanne from behind one day, she's riding him on her desk amidst a pile of papers and spilled coffee and takeout containers the next, then on Thursday he's boning two Kellyannes, her image somehow doubled—*twinz!!*—and then on Friday she's blowing him in front of the whole office, all of them down on their knees, watching in reverence, gasping when he gasps, groaning when he groans, like the mindless, docile puppets he's always known they were.

He's amped up all weekend, like a new man. On Monday morning he goes back to Kellyanne's desk first thing, and stands near her, panting as he looks at the ceiling with a little wink at where he imagines the camera to be. He swaggers off just as she asks him what's up, confident that, come tonight, he'll be watching himself fuck her ragged again, a martini in one hand, his rod-on (he'd been taught to call it this, instead of boner or stiffy, by a thoughtful uncle when he was twelve) in the other, and all will be well.

And he's not wrong, or not entirely. That night he's there at his desk, vid open and rod-on in hand, sipping his martini, ready to watch himself pound her a good one again, same as last week, when, instead of that, he ends up watching her—he can't believe his eyes!—shove him against Mr. Veitch's desk, whip his pants and boxers down, grab a cuke from her lunch bag and, fingering herself down the top of her elastic waistband with one hand, shove him good and hard with the other, ramming the cuke all the way up his butt, which, incidentally, itches and even hurts a bit now, right here where he sits.

He zips his pajamas and orders dumplings and puts what he just saw out of mind, but as the week goes on the vids start showing him down on his knees sucking off Mr. Veitch, or pounding him doggy-style, or taking a pounding, sometimes from two Mr. Veitches, and sometimes from three. Gribby pushes through the shame or fear or whatever he might want to feel about it, and cums again, spilling his martini all over his computer, thinking, *Dammit, now I'm gonna have to buy a new one.* He uses his old computer's dying gasps to get online and buy another, and just as he goes to his email account to confirm the purchase, he sees an email from PornME that he sort of wants to not open. He opens it and it says, "Two weeks down / ???? to go bubba xoxoxo!"

The new computer arrives in no time, and he plugs it in, imagining a million things he might do with it aside from checking his PornMEmail, since what he sees when he checks it makes him none too happy. He has to admit the vids are getting strange. They've moved past regular fucking, and even past gay fucking. Now he's doing things to Kellyanne and his boss and Gerry, this fat guy with rotten skin in accounting, and of course the interns, and now here he is doing something pretty bad to Pamela in HR's daughter, who—though he tries not to look too closely when her face fills the screen (*then again, is it illegal just to look?*)—can't be more than twelve.

He feels himself falling toward the very bottom of the internet, faster and faster. The vids seem to be coming faster now too, *more than one a day*, he thinks, unless it's the days that are going faster, losing their middles, or consisting only of middles, their beginnings and ends snipped off, tending more and more toward the few moments of behavior, however slight, that are captured and then edited by PornME into the vids he's watching now, and now again, and now yet again, and once again, and here's another, and another. Soon, at this rate, he fears he'll find himself old, spent, the bulk of his life lost in some run-off container on the outskirts of the megacity.

Gribby wants to stop vid production because—*why lie?*—he can tell he's about to kill someone if he doesn't. The vids keep getting worse, and he can sense that one day soon he'll be sitting in his stained Ikea desk chair, rod-on in hand, martini at the ready, when what'll he see onscreen but himself throttling Kellyanne to death on her desk, or bashing her face against her monitor until it goes through and stays stuck in there, or pulling a semi-automatic from his tote bag and shooting the whole fucking monkey show to high heaven, chortling like Beavis on his birthday as the ambulance screeches in.

And then, even if everyone's still technically alive the next day, he can tell they'll never again seem like more than ghosts…*not that they ever seemed otherwise anyway.*

"Please please please stop sending 'em," Gribby writes.

He waits, breath held, after he's hit "SEND," only exhaling when the response arrives: "Don't worry, we know u want it bubba xoxoxo!"

He doesn't have the heart to fight them, especially not after all the

18

energy he's put into downplaying how excited he is to see himself manhandling Kellyanne into an early grave and/or kneeling down on Gerry's chest and twisting his face around like a plastic dummy's, which he's watching now, rapt, behind his new twenty-six-inch monitor—they've gotten bigger with each new purchase, and there've been several by now. He watches with the volume down low as he crushes Mr. Veitch's skull and smothers Kellyanne with a plastic bag and, though part of him regrets it even as he's doing it, he presses "PLAY" on the vid again as soon as it's over, and again after that.

"Naughty naughty," comes the response, in red letters over the paused screen. "Just you waity waity big bubba baby boy xoxoxo!"

He knows better than to try clicking it again. He powers off his computer, totally unable to watch any other porn—actually, he hasn't watched any since the very first time he screwed Kellyanne regular-wise in what feels now like some distant teenage love affair. "Stranger porn," he calls it now, scoffing. *Who'd wanna cheat on himself with dirty old stranger porn?* Even the thought of it grosses him out, like finding someone else's pubes on his soap in the shower.

So, all weekend—weekends, when no new vids come in, are the worst—he wanders his apartment, eating dumplings and staring at the empty parrot cage with no memory of its former occupant.

Everyone at work on Monday looks at him with tired, bovine eyes as he settles in behind his desk and thinks, booting up his smaller, inferior work computer, *By six o'clock tonight, I'm gonna be grooving to me killing you all, and there won't be anything you mooks can do about it lol xoxo!*

And sure enough, he's right. He's behind his computer now, rod-on red and bleeding in hand, drinking gin from the bottle, no vermouth, no olives, eyes an inch from the screen as he mows everyone down with an Uzi, blasting them out of their desks, and in some cases, through the shitty, cheap ceiling, bone and plaster flying everywhere, in a cloud so thick he finds himself wiping his screen in hopes of clearing the image.

This goes on all week, or for many weeks, the carnage getting wilder and more baroque—from Uzi to crossbow to sword to switchblade to rusty nail to a big, gooey bag of AIDS blood—until PornME finally crosses what Gribby would still like to consider *The Line*: he's at home on a Friday night, dumplings at the ready beside his computer, when what does he see but the office filling with greenish-yellow gas and everyone coughing, gagging and slumping over in their swivel chairs, faces puffy and wilting, while he—the Gribby onscreen—sits behind his work computer operating a lever that has grown out of his keyboard, a paper party hat strapped to his head and a giant clown smile painted over his mouth.

The vid won't end, and, though the Gribby-at-home presses "PAUSE"—or thinks he's pressing it—it won't stop, either. It just goes on and on, the gassed bodies blowing up like meat left underwater until they pop and, gross as it makes him feel, he finds he's popped as well, so to speak, behind his computer, in the comfort of the apartment he lives in, alone in the heart of the megacity.

He finds himself crying as he polishes off his gin and tucks into his dumplings, the bodies still exploding onscreen, the gas pouring over them, covering the monitor like a screensaver, and he dimly hears himself think, like a child whispering from the far back of his head, *Enough, enough, for the love of God, enough.*

So, in the morning—after falling asleep behind his computer, sauce all over his lap—he opens his email and, though his fingers are sticky and his mind dull, types:

"Dear PornME,

I don't like this anymore. I'm not kidding this time either. Please suspend my service. Bill me through the end of the month or even the year, whatever, I don't care about the money. Just please stop sending them."

He highlights the whole thing and almost deletes it, but manages to swoop in with his other hand and hit "SEND" just in time. Then he breathes long and slow, terrified. *Am I scared of what they'll do to me,* he wonders, *or scared of what I'll do without them?*

He sits there all day, feeling halved without the onscreen Gribby, until, around nightfall—or what he imagines must be nightfall, since his shades are drawn and have been all day, or night, if it's been night all this time—a response comes:

"Dear Gribby,

Hahaha. Ya don't like what yr doing to them? Well how's about we do it to you then? Someone at work, someone on the street, someone who comes to your door, haha…you won't know who it'll be, but they'll know you! Be ready, bubba xoxoxo."

Suffice it to say, next Monday at work isn't Gribby's idea of a good time. He walks, cowed, among his co-workers, wondering which it'll be, the one to shank him in the bathroom or slip strychnine in his Lipton while he's zoned out watching the microwave.

He gets home, already shaking and covered in sweat, and boots up his computer (wishing it were smaller now, the images harder to see) and opens his inbox with the new vid inside. He watches, though he wishes he didn't have to, as Kellyanne corners him by the water fountain (he remembers this interaction from today—they'd discussed AmEx vs. Discover, the futility of earning AirMiles when there was nowhere to go) and stabs him in the throat with a ballpoint pen.

Gribby shivers, disgusted at the scene, and even more disgusted to look down and find he's cum in his lap without even touching his rod-on, like a little kid who shits himself in the sandbox after chugging a box of apple juice at recess. He's too grossed out to order dinner, so he just closes his eyes in his seat and waits.

The waiting goes on until he hears the ping of a new email. He opens one eye, blinking painfully in the glare and opens it: "Welcome to Phase Two, lil' willy. Congrats! Woo-hoo, *laissez les bons temps rouler*!! Xoxoxo."

He clicks the link at the bottom of the page and finds himself watching a vid of himself sitting in his computer chair, shivering, eyes fluttering under closed lids, while a masked figure enters his apartment, takes a paring knife from the wall strip in the kitchen and walks behind him, dragging it over his neck, tickling his gristle without quite drawing blood.

Gribby touches his throat, unsure if he'd rather feel a scratch mark there, and thus know the vid is real, or not, and thus know…*What? That it's all pretend, like it's been all along?*

Months begin to pass, or keep passing, and Gribby can't tell how alarmed he is or should be. It doesn't seem as though anyone's killed him for real yet, though the vids of him being stalked, stabbed and strangled keep on coming.

And he has to pay rent, so he bides his time at work as best he can, trying to keep to himself so as not to be caught on camera with Kellyanne or anyone else anymore, though the vids pour in regardless: now she's feeding him a hot coffee pot, now Mr. Veitch is stapling his nips to the wall, now some pimply temp's Gorilla-gluing his face to the hot glass of the copy machine.

He sits at home watching, trying to remember that it's all just porn, but he keeps looking over his shoulder, double- and triple-checking the locks on the door and even installing new ones, and changing the keys, and installing a new state-of-the-art alarm system, and throwing all his knives and even his spoons and forks and takeout chopsticks in the trash, eating dumplings with his fingers from now on.

Finally, a year or two later, he writes another email:

"Dear PornME,

Again, I'm begging you, please stop. I don't like watching myself get hurt. I was kidding last time, but this time I'm not."

The ping of the response is almost immediate:

"Don't like it? Sure ya do. Don't believe us? We have yr dopamine reports to prove it. We could send them over right now, if ya wanna see 'em, bubba. Just let us know :) xoxoxo."

No, he doesn't wanna see 'em, so he keeps his mouth shut for another few months, or years, his hair slowly falling out, his gut making his rod-on harder and harder to find.

Nothing changes until the day he finally writes, "Okay, I'm gonna come down there and tell ya how I feel in person," and they write, "Sure let's party" and send him an address. So next time Saturday comes around, he gets on a bus, then another bus, then the aboveground tram, then a third bus, making his way to the far outskirts of the megacity. It's a grim warehouse district, full of beached ships and scrap metal, the kind of place that'd make a sane person stop short and say, "Wow, I had no idea this was here."

The day was a total waste, as far as he could tell—he wandered along drafty, paint-smelling halls and found no one at all to talk to, and emerged in late afternoon in the winter dusk. By the time he got home, a vid was waiting. It showed him at the headquarters, throttling a mild-looking bald man, squeezing his throat until the face went purple and the capillaries burst. *The funny thing,* Gribby muses, while stroking himself as the vid plays on, *is I can't tell which of those two men is me.*

Now Gribby works at the office he went to that day. He goes in every morning and sits in the cold dark behind a screen and does nothing, only to come home and watch himself kill customers, or be killed by customers, or both, until a new email arrives:

"Dear Gribby,

At some point, a hand will reach through the screen, or an agent will appear at yr door, and then it will all, at last, become real. Shockingly, terrifyingly real, as all things eventually must. We know neither the day nor the hour, chubchub. Until then, enjoy!

Xoxoxoxo."

Gribby stares at the screen, telling himself that even this is part of the porn, maybe the best part, until another day passes and a new vid arrives. In this one, he's running through hallways of splattered blood and viscera, frolicking like a pagan god, chest huge and red, feet horny and cleft. The next day, the vid shows him running in terror down those same hallways, while the pagan god pursues him, laughing and drinking wine from a goatskin, shouting, "Soon! I'm coming soon! Wait up for me, honey bumbum!"

And the next day he's both at once, the god and its prey, the mouth and the morsel, running up and down the endless halls of the building, which—*who knows?*—perhaps he's worked in all this time, doing what he's always done, selling PornME to suckers wherever they can be found.

So he holds on tight, determined to avoid change at all costs, going to work in that huge, lonely office among the derelict warehouses, and coming home to watch himself frolic and flee, until, one evening, the doorbell rings. Remembering his dumplings, he zips the dick window of his full-body pajamas and gets up to answer it.

In the door stands a man about his age. The man holds a knife. "I found this in the trash outside," he says in a voice that reminds Gribby of his own.

"What are you, um…?" He asks, but by this point he can no longer tell which one he is.

"I'm gonna kill ya no matter what," he continues. Then he removes a phone from his pocket and turns on the camera. "Wanna do it as a shower scene?"

He nods and follows the man in, or leads the man in, and they take their clothes off and get in the shower, and soon the tub is running with blood and one of the men is slumped, dying against the other, who's uploading the vid to a private server with the caption, "Another Gribby down the drain, RIP bubba, xoxoxoxoxoxoxo!!"

GHOST

oor Gribby's on his last legs, dying in the tub with the duplicate Gribby standing over him with his rod-on in one hand and his phone in the other, the footage already live, so that Gribbys the world over can get a sweet, sweet taste of what they've been missing.

Now Gribby's huddled, fetal, stinking the ol' drain up with his dumpling-salty blood and gamey panic sweat, color leaving his skin like a lychee that's soaked too long in ice. He's looking up at the other Gribby, the one he glommed onto in all that porn he watched of himself getting busy with everyone who will now outlive him, when what does that Gribby say but, "Look, you wanna die here like a little hog boy, or you wanna live a little longer and see what happens next? Cuz, what with the state you've let yourself fall into in this here chub-tub of yours, only PornME2 can save you now."

Gribby looks up at him, eyes all swimmy and pupilless, unsure what to focus on, and tries to nod. *Do I wanna die?* he asks himself. *No, I don't suppose I do,* comes the answer. "No, I'm pretty sure I do not," he groans. "Not if you're asking, no, I'd definitely prefer not to, thank ye kindly good sir."

"Well then hoo-ha Sally," says the Gribby-in-his-prime, as he reaches down to insert something under the dying Gribby's left ear. *To be totally honest,* the dying Gribby thinks, *that big fat needle thingy hurts—I'm still a hunk of flesh, not a USB port, am I not?—but given that I've just been stabbed to death in a vicious shower scene, it doesn't hurt all that much in the larger scheme of things, if such a scheme remains.* In any case, the needle pain becomes a moot point as soon as Gribby launches into his spiel, which goes a little something like:

"Okay, so how this works is we keep debiting from the same account we've been debiting from all along—don't worry, it doesn't get shut off after you die as long as there's any juice left in it, which, judging from your most recent statement, if I'm not confusing you with another Gribby, ought to buy you a good while yet—and hey, congrats on that—and we float you through space, the great open void, bubba, the big highway in the sky, the Celestial Realms of the Seven Spheres of the Big Guy's Splooge-o-Rama, hubby bear, if you see where I'm off to with all this, so you can, like, check out all you missed by waiting around on Earth for something to happen."

If my throat weren't slit, Gribby thinks, *I'd nod,* even though he isn't sure he understands what his better half's trying to say. *These things make more sense once they start happening, don't they?* he hopes, sensing that his body's already beginning to drift out of the bathtub, through the ceiling, through the apartments above, through the roof, through the smog blanketing the megacity, through the clouds heavy with acid rain, past a Virgin America flight to Vancouver, through a hole in the atmosphere, and into a blackness so absolute that at first he can't tell if he's still conscious, nor quite what it would mean to discover that he isn't.

He comes to in full drift, neither hot nor cold, neither heavy nor light, caked in blood but no longer bleeding, red and dry as a chili peanut. He feels like a newborn but without the dread of having to live a life. *All I have to do is drift,* he decides, ogling one planet at a time, checking out their smooth curves, their moist, velveteen topographies, *until I finally…*

He's forced to abandon this line of inquiry when the vastness of the moon fills his field of vision and he finds himself tumescent with the revelation that he's a drifting sperm and the moon's a waiting egg. No other thought intrudes until he happens to notice himself blowing out a cloud of hovering jism, which fertilizes the moon, causing it to thicken and sprout with water, greenery and a race of moonlings that proceeds to enslave and exterminate itself until Gribby feels the need to fertilize the now-barren satellite all over again.

Pornhound that he is, he does this over and over, unfathomably often, until he gets bored. Then he drifts deeper into space and does it again elsewhere, and again after that, planet after planet, nebula after nebula, each time titillating himself with the unique rush of becoming the demiurge, the benevolent godhead that breathes life into the coldest crevasses of the universe where, a moment before, there'd been nothing. The process is so erotic that Gribby finds it impossible to imagine how he ever got it up for poor ol' Kellyanne. Compared to this, the naked guys and gals of PornME1 were like millipedes scuttling over sandwiches in a campsite trash can. "Hardly a #partystarter, if you see where my head's at," he mutters, but this time the other Gribby doesn't respond.

Strange eons now begin to pass in the depths of space. So many that Gribby has become the progenitor of every galaxy, all of them fertilized through his furious and meticulous masturbation, growing into their own unique worlds as soon as they come into existence, only to collapse and demand resurrection an astral millisecond later. He floats sometimes with an airy feeling and sometimes with a swimmy feeling, moving through thick space and thin space, into gusts of hot air and tunnels of grueling cold that dead-end in black holes, which suck him in and spit him out, either back to where he started or billions of light-years away. It's fun to guess which it'll be, and to invariably end up wrong, as if the black holes were reading his mind, which, *Ha ha,* he realizes, *they probably are.*

In the millennia during which this slowly dawns on him, Gribby—though he now feels too multifarious to dwell within that name, his essence unfurled from the sausage casing of its earthly selfhood—begins to perceive some unifying presence firming up around him. Out of the shapeless smears of stardust and the purple-blue trails of comets, something invisible yet sentient is beginning to make itself known inside his head; some somber, brooding, inscrutable entity is emitting waves of thought that he can't help but internalize. Soon, they've penetrated so deep into the vaginal folds of his brain that he has the feeling they're coming from him, that they're his thoughts, even though, at the same time, the sense that this entity is vegetating at the very heart of space and sucking him into its maw, like, well, whatever's at the very heart of space, is only growing stronger. *Perhaps,* he decides, *I am beginning the process of being unborn, only to be born again as something colossally greater than anything I could ever have dreamed of being before.*

The notion of being sucked in by the universe and spit back out the other side turns him on like nothing else ever has. More eons pass and more planets are born, though Gribby's role in the process seems to be segueing out of the psychosexual and into the purely biological. *It just keeps happening,* he thinks, or notices space thinking, as he drifts past clusters of planets, whole civilizations roiling upon them, some thick with trees, some drenched in green water or clotted in ice that reflects the light of distant stars, some nothing but jagged piles of rock or shifting densities of vapor. As he passes, he hosts their thoughts, and they host his. These are sometimes wise and laconic, and other times vicious, even sadistic, but the line between them and Gribby is softening to the point where, soon, it'll be nothing but a distant memory. *It's like that feeling near sleep, where one thought leads to the next while eclipsing whatever came before it, so that, from any one thought, it's impossible to remember any other, the effect being that every thought, no matter how banal, takes on the immense gravity of The Only Thought Ever.*

I'll be just one entity drifting through the mind of another, he tells himself, having already forgotten his previous thought, *and, somehow, vice versa as well, each of us containing the other so that any boundary between us will be null, and I will dissolve fully, and permanently, into the Mind of God, which will itself no longer go by that name, or any other, because there will be nothing left to name it, nor to require that it be named, as it goes about its habitual masturbation in peace, creating planets as a sort of by-product of the only process that ever really salved the loneliness of being the All-one, and thereby passed the time, even at the outermost extremities of time, so far out here that the concept has no real meaning, at least not when you're no longer an embodied individual, moving in a straight temporal line from Point A to Point… um…*

Here, on the threshold of his self's irrevocable dissolution and the severing of his last link to any form of existence outside of total oneness with the Entity Formerly Known as God, something deep inside him snorts in protest. Some scared baby homunculus that's desperate to maintain its separation from the unmapped nothingness of the infinite cries out and, like a moan from a vid you thought was on "MUTE," a strain of unbearably mournful blues punctures the otherwise deathly silence of PornME2. As soon as he registers the sound, he begins falling out of orbit, flailing, a strain of terror inflecting the music as he plummets toward the surface of whatever distant planet it's coming from. *One of my babies. One of the infinite sub-Gribbys* (he remembers his name now, too) *lost in the enormity of the real—free, free-falling, until…*

Phew, for a moment there, I lost myself, he thinks, coughing in a cloud of lunar dust and scratching at the implant behind his ear. Back in his body, resurrounded by the familiar dead tissue, the old bum knee, slit throat and dumpling-grease love handles, a briny combination of remorse and relief begins to marinate his soul like those cocktail olives he used to fish from the very back of his fridge.

"Way to kill the mood, dude," whispers the other Gribby in his earpiece, who has also, it would seem, come back online. "Way to harsh the whole mellow midnight vibe we so graciously laid out for you up there, Care Bear. Way to chicken out with your dick out like a day-drunk ballerina!"

Gribby's still working on his comeback when the dust clears and he can see, about fifty feet away, the blues duo whose tune summoned him out of orbit in the first place. The first human forms he's seen in what feels like, and may well be, millions of years. Perhaps the first of all time. He gets to his feet and stumbles toward them, transfixed by the beauty of their jam, one of them on guitar, the other on upright bass, singing in perfect harmony, until he gets close enough to recognize them as Sun Ra and Hitler.

He stands as close as he dares and sways to the tune, unable to think because the music is simply too beautiful. Hitler presses his mustache up to a 50s-style radio mic and wails in German, while Sun Ra lays down a truly celestial bassline, his fingers covering whole octaves with no visible strain. Then he leans in to sing the next verse in what sounds like an extraterrestrial patois, while Hitler finger-picks a heartbreaking series of arpeggios on a vintage acoustic guitar decked out with roses and rhinestone swastikas.

Gribby feels the blues coursing through his newly-restored body, which is growing smaller and denser by the moment, returning to its minuscule human proportions, buried in the kind of internet hole that, he knows, only opens up after dozens of warning signs have been ignored. He feels the full immensity of the space he's traveled through, and, for the first time since he signed up for PornME2 while dying in the shower, he admits that he's lost. He's so far afield that he can't tell whether he's alive or dead, which is not a feeling he's ever had before, not even in the depths of PornME1, back when he lived alone in the heart of the megacity, his pajamas always open at the crotch, a bag of delivery dumplings always at the ready by the cordless mouse in his left hand, near the sweat stain his martini glass left on his particleboard desk.

Unless that, too, was a hallucination, one more porn window open among so many millions that, in aggregate, they made up little more than dots in a photo mosaic of God's grimacing, spluttering face.

In any event, he acknowledges, forcing himself to focus, *I'm homesick. I almost lost myself completely, and now I'm back, but that means…* Before he can decide what that means, Sun Ra and Hitler move on to a new number, equally potent but snappier, zippier. So now Gribby's dancing, trying to suppress his mounting dread at how far he's drifted, distracting himself by noting that *all those stories about how Hitler escaped the bunker in Berlin and ended up in space were true. Goddamn Hitler in space. At least there's no mystery as to why Sun Ra's here.*

The next time he looks up, Sun Ra's blowing into a kazoo, holding it to his lips with one hand and smooshing the mic against it with the other. He winks through the purple darkness and Gribby feels his chest expand, puffed up and sprouting sensitive hair like a werewolf caught alone on a Yorkshire moor under the harvest moon. Soon he's so swollen with music that he breaks into a tarantella. For the first time in his life, he forgets himself to the point where he even forgets that he's forgetting himself. Hours pass in a manic fugue, his feet leaving the dusty planet's surface for whole minutes at a time as he grows more and more aroused until he can't contain his enthusiasm. "Could you ever, lil' blubba-bub-bub?" the earpiece hisses. Riven with sudden shame, he watches himself ejaculate so forcefully that he's blown off this planet and back into space, which now feels emptier than ever before, bereft of all landscape save for the grim Milky Way of his expanding emission.

For many more eons—they seem to come in bulk—Gribby drifts, growing lonely, growing old, the spark that sired planets gone from his loins. The divine presence that he felt before remains diffuse now, indifferent to him, perhaps nonexistent. He begins to wonder if it was ever there, or if, all those eons ago, he'd merely succumbed to his own desire to believe.

Not that I quite succumbed, he remembers, bitterly.

"Bet you wish you did when you had the chance, huh, tubthumper?" The other Gribby cackles in his ear.

Again failing to find a retort, Gribby can't help but agree. "If the chance came again," he admits, "I'd buy-with-one-click and never think twice. But if it never does, then, what's my, like, reason to persevere at this point?"

"You ain't got none, big pun," the implant hisses, and, for the first time since PornME2 began, Gribby's tempted to reach behind his ear and rip the damn thing out.

"Who's to say I don't just give you a nice little tug and send ya flying all by your lonesome through that squid ink out there, and see how you like it?"

"Give it a try, cable guy. Think PornME2's a joke? Go ahead. See how you like the punchline."

Tempted, Gribby's fingers cluster around the rubber coating over the metal slug. "And who's to say I'm not dead already, down in that slimy ol' bathtub of yours, I mean mine, and then what exactly have I been paying for all these years, letting you debit my account like it's a take-whatever-you-want-party-bag, if all this is just regular ol' dead time and there's nothing fancy about it?"

"You tell me, little pickle. But what I'll tell you, since we've apparently reached the point in the party where everyone's just saying the first thing that comes to mind, is that they all say this right about now. All the sneaky little PornME2 Gribbsters like you, they all start thinking about saving a buck by ripping their you-know-whats out, since they might be, you know, dead already, so what's the harm, marm? But you know what the harm is? The actual harm, G-man, if I were to, like, totally level with you? The actual harm is that you can't be sure. You can never be sure that, without PornME2, it wouldn't collapse into total and absolute nothing. The real deal dark baby. Wormtown, USA. Which, compared with the cold void of space is even more, um….actually let me check on that one and get back to you."

Before the implant can gibber any more nonsense, Gribby reaches into his spacesuit, which is just a souped-up version of his old full-body pajamas, and begins to pump his groin, tentatively at first, cooking up the idea in his lower brainstem that he'll rip out the implant at the last moment as a sort of ultimate orgasm, a reverse Big Bang, and go out the way the universe came in. So now he's got one hand on his rod-on and one on the implant, yanking on both like it's his job to squish the God that wouldn't give him a second chance at love.

He's just about to finish when what does he hear but those same blues from before, louder than ever. They enter him just as they did when he was young, Sun Ra and Hitler on their lonely orb, plinking away on their banjos and lap steels, soundtracking purgatory with heartbreaking precision. Gribby's soothed like a fetus in its amniotic slop as the implant whispers, "You touch me again, big spender, and this all turns off, and you wanna know what death's really like? I checked, and it turns out it's exactly like this but silent, totally silent, no blues at all, nor even the memory of any blues, and you wouldn't wanna dance to that, now would you, butter broth?"

Defeated, Gribby's hands sink down to his sides, flap-like, his expression sullen as a chastised toddler's. He drifts through space in search of the music's source, aware that it may, at this point, be no more than a memory. *Still, aren't time and space supposed to be, like, the same thing all the way out here?*

Over the years—or miles—the music reverberates, eclipsing all other memories, merging with the last remnants of the godhead fantasy until the two are one and, together, make up all there is. The memory of that carefree young man dancing the tarantella, leaping through the air like a marionette, is the final legacy of all existence, the diamond that all the carbon in the universe has finally compressed itself into.

He fingers the implant under his ear as proof that he's not really dead, gone forever from the universe he created. Terrified at how close he came to tearing it out, he fondles it now, scratching it, batting at it, feeling all sensation dry up in his groin and pool under his ear until one day, long after his lower body has atrophied and his mind has ceased to produce new thoughts, a voice from the deep past, the age of myth and miracle, resurfaces to say, "Your account is now empty, so your implant is set to self-destruct."

The voice begins to fragment and echo as gluey white foam leaks down Gribby's neck and he roils in a combination of pleasure and pain. "Time is not space, time is money," the voice adds, "and now both have run out. Your complimentary final scene is loading."

The dead space around him judders and jolts as the light dims and the shapes of walls and a ceiling grow out of nothing, quickly simulating the décor of a smoky, Weimar-era nightclub. Gribby's the lone occupant, sipping a martini, watching

Hitler and Sun Ra take their places on the bandstand and begin to play a set just for him, like he's some big-spending Euro VIP in the late 1920s.

At the end of an enchanting hour, they stop and say, in one voice, "For our final number, are there any requests from the crowd?"

And Gribby, addressing someone other than himself for what feels like the first time in his life, says, "Play 'The Root of All Pornography' for me one last time."

They nod, happy to oblige. After Hitler has tuned up a bass and Sun Ra has taken a seat behind an old cabaret piano, they strike up a rambling two-step rhythm and vamp for a few bars. Then they begin to sing, in unison:

> *"There once was a universe,*
> *It was a pretty cozy place.*
> *There once were some people,*
> *They danced with joy and grace.*

*There once was a blue-green planet
Earth,
But now, poor Grib',
It's just you in outer space."*

Gribby finds he's tapping and singing along as the song reaches the chorus:

*"The root of all pornography,
The root of all pornography,
The root of all pornography is this:
That anything at all, anywhere,
Ever used to exist."*

Unable to imagine the song ending, he shouts through his slit throat, "Encore! Encore! Play it again!"

For the moment, Sun Ra and Hitler keep singing, so Gribby springs to his nerveless feet, knocking his martini over as he reprises the tarantella he danced all those millennia ago. His body's creakier and slower now, his eyes milky and his hearing shot, but his spirit's free as he reels around and around the slowly vanishing room. He throws his hands in the air and whips his atrophied legs in frantic circles, his pajamas drenched in sweat and open at the crotch as he jigs like a newborn satyr, determined not to stop until there's literally nothing left of him.

FATHER

ext thing he knows, Gribby, or some heavily processed by-product thereof, lands real hard on a soggy bottom under a hot wax roof and splats in the muck and says, "Phew."

He looks around, wishing he didn't have to but sensing that he probably does, and sees that wherever this is ain't none too pretty. *If I talked like that, he thinks, that's just what I'd say. I'd say it's a dank, sweaty cavern with heat wafting down and the screams—the beggings*

*of numerous sorry twerps for mercy—
wafting up, colliding right in the spot where
I'm sitting now.*

No more Weimar nightclub; no
more show tunes, by the looks of it.

He sits, groaning in the muck,
and feels his ragged space suit unravel,
revealing two withered thighs framing
ten spindly pubes, the skin around his
shaft peeled back and blistered from eons
of hard living. He bats it side to side,
wondering if any response is still latent. It
looks like a fossil in a dry lakebed,
juxtaposed against whichever thigh it
happens to land on. *The steering apparatus
on this particular ship is busted,* he admits,
sounding much more alone in his head
than he would've chosen to, had anyone
solicited his preference. *I sound like a
captain shouting to a crew that's long ago
gone ashore.*

Or drowned.

"I hope you all drowned!" he
barks, and his voice echoes in the cavern,

the reverb tinny, the loneliness effect cheap and obvious.

If only I could taunt myself with a modicum of conviction, he wishes, a moment later, as two bats trailing clouds of purloined data swoop down and suck him up, shoving his head deep into their maws—two furry cavities of no certain dimension. First one, then the other, then together, the two cavities revealing themselves to be two chambers of the same larger, er…now they're flying him over scorched and crinkled earth, the smell of sweat so profuse he assumes it's the place itself that's squirting it up. "Calm down, man," he urges the hellscape, while, at the same time, his voice all hellish in his head, he thinks, *It's you that needs to calm down, lil' Gribbins. You're stressing everyone out here.*

"Say, isn't this all a little chintzy?" he mumbles, as soon as the bats drop him in what he takes to be their lair, the ground itchy with dander. "I mean, I thought you guys were basically mammals and so, like…bound by precedent? I mean," he tries to remember the term, "human rights?"

They hiss and chatter while biting his left ear off.

He wonders which one did it and finds that he can't tell. This, more than the bite itself, juices him silly with fear. He looks between the two bats and watches them gnaw and cackle and chew and hack and spit and gnaw and cackle again, sucking down what's surely more meat than one ear can hold, and he finds that, no matter how many times he tries, he just can't nail down which is which. *Maybe losing that ear has made me… lopsided,* he worries, as his eyes mist over and the two bats—or the one bat, the wombat—finish chewing and finally swallow. And then they come, or it comes, after his other ear, and so now he's got none, which leaves him to wonder just what, if anything, has

become of the PornME2 implant that's
gotten him this far.

Sometime later, after what he
decides to consider a sort of
mock recovery period, the smooth-
headed, earless Gribcritter hustles away
from the satiated bat, or bats, and
down a steep, craggy cliff, headfirst, no
longer caring if he crashes and burns at
the bottom.

The bottom, it turns out, is a
concept better suited to an earlier time.
Now, he falls and falls, past geysers of
scum and cascades of guano, until he
finds himself standing, with no tangible
sense of ground underfoot, in a pile of
sweatsuits, all of them roughly modeled
on the foot pajamas that used to be his
uniform.

*And what am I now, naked or
something?* he wonders, afraid to try
looking down. "Oh, just try!" he orders

himself. So he does, wrenching his neck with excruciating sharpness on a swivel that clearly doesn't want to turn, like he broke his spine in the fall even though there was no impact to speak of, and he may be falling still.

"Happy now?" he asks, but receives no reply. The alterna-Grib, as it were, that once burbled so sweetly, or even not so sweetly, in his ear, is offline. *The Grib-faced bat that used to hang from the roof of my skull,* he begins, determined to extract some metaphorical value from the otherwise senseless encounter he's just suffered, *has flown the, um…coop?*

With nothing to hold him back, he begins traipsing through the piles of pajamas, some wetter than others, some sprouting roughage. The field appears infinite, but Gribby can sense, however hazily, that if he doesn't keep moving, an edge of some kind will begin to close in on him. An edge, or a set of edges. *Bad place to be whatever the opposite of a moving target is*, he thinks, extricating his feet from the puddle-like fuzz of one set of PJs and moving on, trying to keep his orientation on the distance fixed, even as the sweat or sperm he's walking through begins to grow fur around his ankles.

He runs through a cluster of yard signs that all read, "AND WHAT FRESH HELL IS THIS?" and keeps running, uncertain whether the pain building up in his feet is trying to get through to the rest of him. If it is, it's doing a pretty weak job of it, though he can't shake the dread that it's all going to hit at once. He only hopes that the growing fur will provide, at the very least, a buffer of sorts. *A shunting of the sharpest aspects of human terror down into the presumably duller depths, or shallows, of bestial resolve,* he muses, a little high on his own unexpected eloquence.

In this state of mind, he dead-ends against the chrome side of a heaving, sixties-style HP mainframe. He looks up at it, and it looks down at him, or at least it doesn't look away, and he reaches for his crotch—which he hereby dubs the wound area—in hopes of bolstering a unified front against what he can tell is a vicious machine that feels no pity for mankind. *The heart of the heart of the program,* he thinks, impressed by the relative ease with which he found it. *Though to be fair, PornME never was a quest game. Attainment-through-ordeal has hardly ever been the point.*

Anyway, he continues, as if dismissing a heckler, *this is the center of the maze. The nexus of the whole damn thing.* Despite how heady the notion sounds, his wound area responds only by flaking away further beneath his fingers, like a bar of soap left under a dripping shower head.

He falls to his knees with his handful of skin outheld, waiting for a response, which comes at last in the form of the scene simply…pausing. A glitch in the onward flow of ones and zeros. The machine makes no response except to stand firmly in place, self-possessed, effortlessly divine.

Unable to bear his newfound proximity to such power, he stands up, thereby causing the scene to resume, and feels something soft but heavy land on his left foot. As he looks down, he feels the same thing happen again, but this time on his right foot. Hoping to kill two bats with one stone, he bends over, still queasy thanks to his missing ears, and picks up both of his testicles.

Cradling them in his palm like the unhatched eggs of some extinct species of—"I get it already!" he shouts to himself, while wondering if bats really do hatch from eggs—the mainframe comes to life. A hood winks upward in its side and the neon blue outline of a box appears, into which, Gribby doesn't need to be told, he's meant to deposit the former jewels of the family he never had.

His fingers tremble as they approach the churning guts of the PornME apparatus, *the generative hole at the origin of everything, deeper and darker and wetter than all of its fleshy mortal analogues combined.*

Once sated, the box makes a canned gulping sound and then dims back into the mainframe, stranding Gribby right where he's been all this time. For another long, long period, a new batch of nothing plays out. The air continues to smell like sweat, gusts of hot keep alternating with gusts of cold, and black smudges fly in circles around what is presumably meant to be the sky, though it's so free of perspective that Gribby finds it impossible to tell whether they're small, nearby ravens, or giant, distant bats. *Couldn't I have conjured something more vivid? Some hell tied more closely to the life I lived, the mistakes I made, the scores I left unsettled?* He tries, for a grueling moment, to imagine what these might be.

He draws a blank, and then another blank, and then a third. Then he puts the deck away.

Still, the number three hangs in the air. *So long as I was running, or even just wading through pools of offal and eddies of effluvium,* he explains to himself, *it all seemed kinda promising, like this was just the early stages of PornME3, the sequel to the sequel, the final nightmare, a ranker, funkier version of PornME's 1 and 2. A seamier module for today's jaded youth.*

But now he looks up at the silent mainframe and the circling bats or ravens—unless, in fact, they're planets—his head oozing in sympathy with his wound area, and, for the first time, it starts to feel very much like PornME3 is a different beast entirely, or, indeed, no beast at all. Part of no story, a sequel to nothing. *Didn't they say something a while back about my money running out?* He tries to remember.

As the fur creeps up his legs and into his center, he finds himself praying that PornME's running on credit now, racking up a bill which, even with interest, he'll be all too happy to find a way to settle.

Soothed by this prospect, however improbable, he rummages in his wound area, but, newly a gelding, he finds that nothing is primed to occur. This surprises him, despite his knowing all too well that it shouldn't, so he sits down in a field of mussel shells and stares at the blinking mainframe and the crackling sky and faces, once again, the possibility that it all ends here.

A dangerous thought to put into words, he finds, because now the background is swarming in, the distant darkness coming closer. *Closure of the most suffocating kind, the kind that makes claustrophobics of even the most…the most…uh…*he tries to decide what the opposite of a claustrophobic might be, but draws yet another blank. *It's like the difference between a coffin and the clanking hulk of this mainframe and the, um…no, it's more like the difference between these mussel shells and a bunch of, ah…*

He scans the visible spectrum, but finds that no two things are different enough to make the comparison, nor can he remember what comparison he'd been trying to make. It starts to seem as though everything he can see, smell, touch and even think is made of the same base matter, a thick gruel that's no longer partitioned into forms that even appear distinct.

It is what it is, he thinks, though even this seems doubtful. *Either way, maybe this is really it*, he goes on thinking, in hopes of changing the subject, while fearing that this is the very subject he'd been trying to change.

He feels himself begin to float in unrendered space, with nothing touching him on any side except for the fur that's now covered his torso. He closes his eyes and tries to summon the voice that once whispered from the innermost crevices of his brain. "Taunt me," he begs it, "tell me I'm a grub, a custard boy, a little blister baby…" But the voice tells him none of these things, and the blackness only grows blacker.

"'Member when you killed me in the shower and I…I…I? Anyone? Can anyone hear me? Charge me double, I'll find the money, I promise!" In the absence of a response, the hellscape fades into stock imagery, clip art dredged up from the ruins of a collapsed empire. He squeezes his eyes shut and begs for deliverance into a hell of his own making, if hell must be his fate. And yet this, too, strikes him as a cliché, as the phrase "GRIBBY'S DE PROFUNDIS" scrolls across the bottom of his vision, like a title card in a silent film.

After his De Profundis fizzles into bathos, he looks up and notices that his testicles are being unwound in the darkness, all their densely compacted strands wriggling back into the fiber of the universe, and he allows himself to believe that, somehow, his prayer has been answered. *I finally understand string theory,* he boasts, unafraid to sound a little smug, given the circumstances. *I've earned at least that much, haven't I??*

No one disagrees.

He watches the strands wrap themselves into the shapes of planets and stars and tracts of asteroid dust, and he pictures a younger Gribby up there, just beyond view, jigging to the dulcet tunes of Sun Ra and Hitler. The image either remains impacted in his brainstem, or develops for the first time now, pre-soaked in nostalgia, another holdover from the back pages of some long-defunct website. He looks up at the stars as he begins to whisper to the version of himself that he imagines is still up there, "It's not over…it's not over…it's not over just yet."

The work of whispering these lines, set to a rudimentary rhythm, depletes the last of his breath. *Perhaps I can't hear my own reply because I have no ears,* he reasons, as he crawls out of space and onto the edge of an office chair he finds tipped on its side in the murk of the mainframe's shadow, which has stood there unmoved all this time. He rights the chair and, perched on its cushion, leans his arms onto the soft particleboard surface of a desk that has appeared in front of him, and, groping in the dark for an additional prop, pulls a headset over his skull, adjusting the cushioned leather speakers so they cup his weeping earholes with a modicum of tenderness.

Everything feels primed to begin.

He clears his throat and fiddles with the dials on the console at the end of the wire that runs from the bottom of the left headphone to the…console. He laughs. "I just said that, didn't I?" It's a relief to hear his own voice, however faintly. *Proof of life*, he tells himself, uncertain whether this is a common phrase or one he's just coined.

It seems clear, at this point, that talking is the thing to do.

"So," he begins, looking up at the overhanging blackness, "this one's for you, ol' Grib. There was a time, not so long ago, when I was dead to myself. I really believed, if you can believe it, that the whole PornME cycle had played itself out. I lost faith. I sort of, how would you put it? Lost the will to get it up."

He gropes around in his wound area, working up the courage to believe that some response is once again possible. Fingering the slowly regrowing organ, and trying not to ask himself whether it, too, is a prop, he goes on, "You see, Grib, it all began when you lived alone in the megacity, spending your days sealed in an office in the heart of a corporate campus, your nights in front of a screen in your foot pajamas, unzipped at the crotch, an order of dumplings at the ready by your left hand, while your right hand…"

It's working! he thinks. He feels something taking shape under the particleboard desk, an idea firming up in his nerveless fist while a new set of testicles emerges from the cavity of his lower torso, as he goes on and on remembering, or inventing, the other Gribby, the poor Gribby he used to be, alone in the heart of the megacity, clinging to the faint blue thrill of the very first PornME, in an earlier era that had, at the time, seemed as late as any era could get.

"And you came to like it. You came to like it a lot," he says, raising his voice over the din of Sun Ra's bassline and Hitler's sinuous lament. "You came to like it so much that it scared you, and then you came to like being scared, and then you…"

He breaks off here to climax. Though nothing tangible is yet produced, he feels, like a seventh grader at coed swim practice, that great and frightening things lie just ahead.

In the deflating interregnum that follows, however, he sits back at the desk and looks up at the smeared sky, or ceiling, and fears, once again— everything has the draggy slowness of repetition now, like each step forward only loops him back to where he began—that the Gribby he just conjured is returning to numen, dissolving into a bout of wishful thinking drifting through the firmament of a dead man's head, which he pictures now as a sort of equal-opportunity host, willing to run any program that installs itself.

Despondency settles so hard upon him that he falls out of his desk chair and into the muck, which reeks of ancient mussels and seaweed. He begins to sink in as the "GRIBBY'S DE PROFUNDIS" title card creeps back across the bottom of his vision, tentatively, as if afraid that last time it came too soon.

A pause, and then: "A good place to get some thinking done," quips a voice in his head. "Little Chuppa-Chupp, xoxoxoxo." He grins so wide his throat fills with black sludge.

The voice is back online. The game's back on. "That's right, little shrimp vein, you know what you deserve!"

He smiles harder and crawls back to his knees, which he manages to remain balanced on after a third try, and then from his knees he tips into the desk chair, which has sunk so low its seat now rests on the ground, like a kickboard on the surface of a kiddie pool. He reaches

into his furred-over crotch and unzips
the front seam of what appears to be a
brand-new set of full-body pajamas,
having grown organically from his
withered skin. He feels a delicious blend
of pleasure and pain as he drags the
zipper along a fresh nerve ending that
runs between teeth made of fine bone.

Then, shoving the headset back
onto his head, he says, "Alright tubby
Gribbster, I'm comin' for ya, up from the
deep, for real this time."

And cum he does. Over the
next batch of eons, Gribby
works without surcease to build the
megacity from scratch, pouring himself
into the mainframe in thick gouts,
stuffing its circuitry with every idea he's
ever had.

He builds the streets and
buildings and office parks in which the
other Gribby, the lesser Gribby, will

work, and he stocks a series of freezers with a lifetime supply of dumplings and soy sauce and imbues the world with a sense of history and even a sense of destiny, though he knows this may be overkill, and he creates two new testicles from the unspooled detritus of those that used to be his own, which he attaches to the prototype he's slowly conjuring, just as he also conjures a Kellyanne and a Mr. Veitch.

At the same time, he scrapes the bottom-most sludge of his memory and conjures an office complex for himself—a series of dim, drafty hallways, locked rooms full of boxed documents and wheezing desktops, a cafeteria that serves sweaty pasta with meat sauce and orange juice from concentrate in cardboard cartons, a whole business apparatus where, because he's the only one present, his orders are followed without question.

When everything's ready, he puts the headset back on, cranks up "The

Root of All Pornography," and begins to compose an email.

After ten aborted drafts, some as long as five pages and others as short as five words, he gets it right. Rereading it one last time, he closes his eyes and presses "SEND" on a message that reads, "We're watching ya all the time anyway, at work and home and everywhere and stuff, so why not pay a lil' extra to have yr vids porned up, bubba xoxo?"

The waiting period is interminable. Gribby sits at his desk breathing in and out in ragged sighs, zipping and unzipping his flesh pajamas as his lure drifts untended in the waters of eternity. He checks the office clock and sends a few follow-up emails, but can't keep himself from thinking that, if no one responds, it'll be the end of everything. *The end of the end of the end of the end. Over before it began.* His eyes mist up as he pictures an ending in which there never was a PornME, and thus never a PornME2, let alone a

PornME3, meaning that... *I'm what? A ghost? A sentient nonentity?* He chews his knuckles and plays with his nerve zipper and worries. *I've failed to create a world that any real Gribby can inhabit. There is no recourse now, there is no—*

Meanwhile, down in the megacity, Gribby happens to discover an email in his spam folder that intrigues him, far more, if he's honest, than any of those in his so-called normal inbox. He likes porn as much as the next chump, and more especially, he figures, the kind made of vids of him and his co-workers—there's this gal Kellyanne he's always been kinda into, for one thing—so, *what the hell,* he figures, *sure, why not pay $12.99/mo. and see if they can really, as they claim,* "Send ya one sexy vid per weekday featuring you and whoever ya been caught on camera with, rendered so realistically yll swear you were there, which, come to think of it, haha, ya kinda were bubba ya know what I mean xoxo!"

So he inputs his credit card and waits open-mouthed for confirmation to arrive. Then he washes his hands, though they're not exactly dirty, and spills out the Ovaltine he forgot to drink and flushes his dead guppies down the toilet and chucks the tank to the curb after he walks out the door of the apartment he lives in alone except for a parrot named Graham—his own real name, from back before kids started calling him Gribby in the seventh grade, a slight step up from Goblin, which they called him before that, back when he was chubby—and up the street, down to the subway, and back up to another part of the same street and along it to the office he works in with a bunch of ugly and a few sexy people like, as he probably already mentioned, Kellyanne and Mr. Veitch, his boss, a pretty toned and tan older dickhead Gribby can't help but admire.

"Ah," Gribby sighs, spurting for real this time across his already-soggy particleboard desktop somewhere in the deep, hot depths of PornME3. "We got a live one here. Just when I was about to cut bait, the little guppy swallowed the sinker." *You'll never know, Gribby,* he thinks, *how grateful I am for your company because, as you'll soon find out, nothing turns me on more than seeing you scared!*

After wiping his hand on his thigh, he leans over the console and types, "Don't worry, we know u want it bubba xoxoxo!"

Then, trembling with excitement at what he senses is the beginning of a long and fruitful symbiosis, he hits "SEND" and exhales as the message speeds on its way, along a route he can barely imagine, into a brain he knows almost as well as the quivering head of his own resurrected—

he resurrects the term here, as well—rod-on.

This arrangement takes its course, tracing the steadily darkening arc of Gribby's arousal. The Gribby in PornME3, ensconced in the office complex on the far, forgotten edge of the megacity, where barely any buses go, feels the embrace of the new symbiosis close in, like a second womb, better than the first because he can tell that this one is terminal. It will never expel him into a world of cold ambiguity, in which he'll be forced to fend for himself as an individual. His joy at letting go of this fear is immense. He feels sheltered from any urge to consider what might lie beyond, the possibility that all of this is, for the first time, real, that the eons of simulation are over and that they have ended here, on the lip of something so new it must be experienced blind, without a name.

No, he thinks, beginning to draft a new email. *No, PornME3 is still going strong, and whatever lies beyond it might as well be nothing because, even if a door between me and it opened up, I would never go through. I'd rather not know.*

He watches Gribby's $12.99/mo. accrue in the account he's created to receive it, the balance rising and rising, a nest egg to be saved until the day when, at last, his own PornME3 bill comes due, with interest. *Then*—his thoughts drift toward the far future—*I'll be all too happy to pay up, and thus know, at last, that my hard work in this dank, Lipton-reeking office was worth it.*

A blast of heat from the mainframe startles him, and he looks down to see that he's typed the above ruminations into the email window he was about to send to Gribby. "Please, help me remain convinced that it's all still pretend," he watches himself continue, unable to stop, throbbing with excitement at the possibility of scuttling the whole setup, just as he used to throb with excitement at the possibility of another Grib showing up at his door with a knife in one hand, and a phone in the other, ready to shoot a shower scene. "Please do your part to help me blot out the possibility that hell is real and I am in it alone!"

Like so, a third Gribby, a lovechild of the first two, slouches onto the scene, a deeper deviant than either of his fathers, titillated at the prospect of crashing the system, so recently established, and taking his chances with whatever exists outside. He's well aware that this might be nothing at all, or a world of porn-free hurt, and finds this prospect so delicious that he can't help pounding the mainframe for ten full minutes, denting its cooling system and fraying a girthy cable. At the sight of this, the second Gribby, who had, until now, seen himself as the last in the sequence, the final arbiter manning the controls, suddenly feels vestigial, like a mere step in an evolutionary process he can now see extending far, far beyond him, and he thrills—in what might be his final conscious instant—to behold the possibility that even here, within the dreary corporate offices of PornME3, life finds a way to persist, growing ever upward and outward, crashing every system that tries to run it, spoiling all possible symmetry, scuttling every scheme to earn $12.99/mo., until...

After he cums, he exhales and begins to simmer down, letting go of his vision, thinking, *Phew, whoever wrote this program really thought of everything. It's quite a relief to be encased in a world that contains its own outside.* He lets go of the third, somehow satanic Gribby, and resumes the now-familiar process of writing to the first, the little flubberhumper in his foot pajamas in the heart of the megacity, his dumplings cooling on his sauce-stained mousepad. "We gonna chub you up real nice in yr greasy lil tubby-wumpus onesie xoxoxo," he types, trying not to look over his shoulder as he hits "SEND." *No, he insists, there's no one else here. There's just me and you, lil' Gribbins, jerking ourselves onward through one eternity after another, until every last sun burns out and we climax together, along with the universe…and then...and then…*

The prospect of what might come next sends tremors through his body, spasms of fear so dramatic that the third Gribby appears behind him once again, pajamas unzipped, one hand on the back of the office chair while the other goes to work. He tries to pace himself so as to enjoy the full course of his father's descent into madness, the terror of not knowing if he's inside or outside the edifice he's constructed, but as he jerks himself toward fruition, a yet-deeper voice, that of PornME4 perhaps, begins to whisper inside him. It whispers, "You too, whichever Gribby you are, are dead meat. We're coming for you too, we're on our way to yr place, and when we get there, we're gonna…we're gonna…well, heh heh, you'll see. Trust us on that."

This Gribby, whichever one he is, cums on the back of the office chair of the Gribby in front of him, as the voice crackles in his head, whispering, "We're gonna make ya wait for it, lil' knob gobbler…we're gonna make ya beg to find out how it ends, and yr gonna love us soooo much for it, yr gonna luv begging and begging and begging, u just know yr gonna! U never could say no. Bye 4 now bubba, xoxoxoxo."

AFTERWORD

THE BASTARDING GENIUS OF DAVID LEO RICE

BY CHRIS KELSO

My maiden expedition into the territory of David Leo Rice's fiction was not the satirical Ballardian doom lit of *Drifter: Stories*, nor was it the gravelly little noir parables found in both *Dodge City* volumes. No, it was the strange and smutty novella you hold in your hands now. *The PornME Trinity*.

But let's go back to 2020, when it emerged in its first incarnation: we're stuck in the heart of a worldwide lockdown. Authors and independent publishers are doing their part to offer aid, sending out community care packages by the hundred-weight to toiling writers and readers around the globe in a gesture of mass solidarity and togetherness. David kindly sent me a double-walled cardboard box thick with books, and his kindness stays with me to this day. Among the mound inside was a copy of *The PornME Trinity*. I was initially struck by the utterly grotesque cover design, featuring a pastiche of George Méliès' *A Trip to the Moon*, where a sinister lunar body blinks teardrops of semen alongside an untethered astronaut. It's a striking, baffling image, but even that couldn't prepare me for the striking, bafflingly hilarious and downright vulgar peregrination towards a Cronenbergian transcendence that *PM3* had in store. Which brings me to the second thing I love about this book.

It starts with the simple spamming of a naïve young cipher called Gribby. *Side note: I think we can all agree that the idea of a porn-focused book being set in a surveillance society is deliciously fitting.* You see, the PornME company, whoever they are, makes personalised deep fake videos and Gribby, being the creepy wee incel he is, decides to shell out a few extra quid to have one made of him and his co-worker Kellyanne *habens sexus*.

We are all Gribby. Any sensitive young man worth his search history has a darker voyeuristic inner-self that lives a life of stifled frustration—this includes committed altruists like David and me. That is, until a sacred, private moment allows the sick twin to finally be indulged. But, as *PM3* will show you, when you blindly indulge the dormant pervert within, there can only be dire consequences to your perception of external reality.

Rice is an aesthete, a witty and totally urbane individual who looks like he was genetically engineered to teach creative writing classes at The New School. Success follows him. Yet, what I love most about this book you hold in your hands is that it reveals an adolescent playfulness to David's writing personality, on a level you perhaps wouldn't expect from such a kind, measured and scholarly fellow.

Gribby starts to gain traction as a pornographer and, in truly prescient fashion, starts losing control of his own content. While reality literally dissolves around him, Gribby's hold on his own carnal desires and his quest for sexual gratification begin to devolve to the most heinous depths of bad taste and snuff enactment. Gribby is the quiet sex-sick twin occupying our private gonadiccosmos. Just imagine he escaped the empathic exterior. Imagine you were allowed to exist in an unfiltered world of your own creation.

The PornME Trinity is a smart and shocking work that makes me professionally jealous and fraternally proud of Rice. The genius bastard that he is…

Our own world is becoming increasingly over-saturated, to the point of persecution. It's clear that the old way, of logging off and on, is ending and a new period of total immersion/total experience is just beginning. It's a Cronenbergian notion that the media is a sentient entity that wants us to leave this world behind. It's pleading with us to envelop ourselves in the pure pleasure of relentless, infinite content. It was after reading *The PornME Trinity* that I knew Rice was the right man to co-edit our Cronenberg anthology, *Children of the New Flesh*, released in the summer of

2022. Because, really, it is Rice who is our heroic pervert "embodying both the high priest and the sacrificial lamb," as he wrote in the introduction to that book. He is the man in possession of the bravery and authority to succumb to the third alternative, a mystical space hidden between logging on and logging off. Whatever that may be.

Chris Kelso
Glasgow, 2022

Chris Kelso is a British Fantasy Award-nominated genre writer, illustrator and anthologist. His work has been published in *3:AM Magazine*, *Black Static*, *SF Signal*, *Dark Discoveries*, *The Scottish Poetry Library*, *Invert/Extant*, *Sensitive Skin*, *Evergreen Review*, *Verbicide* and many others. He has been translated into French and is the two-time winner of the Ginger

Nuts of Horror Novel of the Year in 2016 for *Unger House Radicals* and in 2017 for *Shrapnel Apartments*. The latter was endorsed by Dennis Cooper via his blog article, "4 Books I Read Recently and Loved."

INTERVIEW

*The following interview was conducted between **The Opiate** and **David Leo Rice** in March of 2020, just as the U.S. was reconciling with its own lockdown fate. One that it seemed to think itself impervious to despite Asia and Europe leading the way on then-unprecedented measures designed to* "stop the spread" (which, of late, doesn't seem to have been stopped at all). As The PornME Trinity addresses an array of topics and motifs that have unfortunately become "evergreen" in our post-Empire existence, looking back on how the novella came to be (not entirely surprisingly, a reaction to the 2016 election), as well as how it would unwittingly evolve into something even more prescient than it was before, Rice's words in this interview offer a far eerier and more premonitory feel with the benefit/detriment of hindsight in 2022.

***

While the times are inarguably grim, and dystopian literature suddenly seems all too real, the strange relevance of one of The Opiate Books' first published works on the imprint, The PornME Trinity, is perhaps a more cautionary tale than ever as we move into forced self-quarantine. Below we discuss everything from the genesis of the project to the advent of coronavirus fetish porn.

The Opiate: *Can you tell us a bit about the genesis of this project? Was it all helmed from a porn-fueled night of boredom or mere commentary on modern society?*

David Leo Rice: It really came to me in the aftermath of the 2016 election, where I felt myself spiraling down a bottomless "news-hole." For the first time, I was physically desperate for data, as if one more tweet, one more think piece, one more podcast could explain and soothe my feelings about what had happened. Or maybe I had reached an even more animalistic level: it wasn't that I had any mental expectations about what this data would reveal, it was that my body craved it as much as food and water. My mind was irrelevant to the process.

I started to suspect that this response was in line with the forces that had caused that election in the first place; it felt like the completion of some process by which screens and entertainment had cannibalized reality, allowing us to elect someone whose only qualification was being entertaining onscreen, and whose main goal seemed to be to promote disregard for any reality outside the one he constructed. I felt terrified of what might happen to whatever reality did still exist outside of that, yet also numbed by the assurance that, no matter what it was, I would only ever experience the consequences through a screen—and, as such, would gulp them down as more data, and be grossly satisfied.

At the same time, I found myself both fearing and longing for something beyond this: some traumatic event that would break through the screen, just as the trauma of the election had pulled me so deeply into it. So, when I started this story, porn was elevated into a complete mode of being, a sense of treating the real, even at its most intense and upsetting, as just more images to consume, while wondering if there could ever be an end to that state, or if it could incorporate its own end and thus prove eternal, rendering us all undead.

The Opiate: *Was it always your intention to build the narrative out into three installments? Or was there something about Gribby's character that kept calling back to you, begging you to give him more pain?*

David Leo Rice: I wrote the first one in a fugue of panic, as I was watching my attention spiral down the rabbit hole. It was really a means of trying to rescue my ability to write, by shunting my worst fears about my own lack of control onto

Gribby. He was like a voodoo doll, absorbing my disgust at my own inability to disconnect from the churning meat grinder of the internet.

The other installments came later, each about a year apart, as I realized that they could form a grander narrative. They were based on the strangeness of the feeling that the world seemed to be constantly ending, but hadn't yet actually ended—this is why Gribby's own death is fed to him as just one more flavor of porn. It's a state I call "unworkable equilibrium," wherein everything feels totally out of balance and yet it spirals inward rather than outward, toward a new and perhaps even more intractable form of balance. Our lives feel permeated by fear and strangeness, but most of us are still able to go on living, perhaps even against our will—most of the conspiracy theories in the 2020s center on various groups and interests having too much control, even as the larger narrative is that of everything flying out of control. The tension between these two poles drove the later parts of the trilogy, or trinity.

I did want to subject Gribby to more and more pain, yet I also wanted to see if I could follow his narrative through to some redemption, even if only a porn-ified, pseudo-redemption. He exists beyond salvation, yet he does undergo a hero's journey between the first and third installment, with the second as a reflecting line or limbo between them.

The Opiate: Considering that the dystopia you depict in the book is already pretty much here, what boundaries, if any, do you think porn has left to push? And, speaking of, how do you feel about the fact that there's already coronavirus fetish porn available?

David Leo Rice: I don't know if porn has any moral boundaries left to push. I suppose they're all technological at this point, in terms of how immersive VR porn can and will become. What's most interesting to me is how non-sexual forces, like climate change and war and political collapse, are also consumed as a kind of porn, stimulating us in this queasy middle zone where we know they're real and yet still perceive them as fake. Classic sexual porn is the opposite: we know it's fake (in terms of its emotions, anyway), yet we try to perceive it as real.

In terms of coronavirus fetish porn, that doesn't surprise me at all. Building off of artists like William S. Burroughs, J. G. Ballard and David Cronenberg, I think there's both beauty and horror in fetishizing disease and even death in this way. On the one hand, it's obviously a callous response to something that may claim a great many lives; on the other hand, it shows the ever-evolving nature of human sexuality, which is at root a life force. Our reproductive instinct is awakened by the prospect of our own demise, a fact that has some poetry to it.

And it's fascinating to note that this seems to happen automatically: though I'm sure there are real people behind the production of coronavirus porn, it feels like an emergent principle, like the world naturally porn-ifies itself as it goes along, and humans are only here to lap it up. The most interesting question to me, if we think about fetishizing our own doom (a process that all apocalyptic thinking, no matter how justified, partakes of—the end of the world isn't called the "Rapture" for nothing) is whether this is a means of accepting death's immediacy, or of further denying it. This is the essential question of porn itself: are we aroused by certain images because they connect us to a reality we're otherwise excluded from, or because they release us from the reality we're otherwise imprisoned in?

The Opiate: With regard to how intimacy is essentially a thing of the past, do you feel that a dependency on screens and porn has made actual human touch more or less devoid of meaning and importance?

David Leo Rice: I don't know if all intimacy is dead, though I do think humanity is going through a transformation, wherein our instinct to reproduce is diminishing, probably for good reason in terms of the planet's health. I don't yet buy into the whole "we're evolving into computerized beings" theory, but there's no doubt that our sexuality is evolving away from one another, and toward digital spaces. It's evolving inward, and perhaps somehow more than inward—like through ourselves and toward a space beyond our own subconscious, which we can't yet accurately name.

What interests me about porn in the 2020s is the question of whether we use it to imagine sex with other humans, or whether we actually use it to have real sex with the computer. How much is it a fantasy of taboo or out-of-reach human contact—which so much contemporary conspiracy thinking, perhaps rightly, fears is being taken from us by governmental and corporate/tech interests that are determined to create a society of total isolation and bottom-up dependence— and how much is it a genuinely new kind of sex act?

The Opiate: What's your take on porn-induced erectile dysfunction? Is it mere myth or does it hold weight in terms of men being desensitized to the sight of a "normal" IRL woman?

David Leo Rice: I'm sure it's possible. In general, I think we're developing an aversion to anything that comes to us unmediated. We've gone so far through the looking glass that screens now make reality real, rather than abstracting it into a second-order version thereof. It's like the tweet confirms the event now, or even generates the event, rather than the event confirming or generating the tweet—in a terrifying way, it almost doesn't make sense to talk about "fake news" anymore, as we now only believe what we read, not what we see. If we meet someone IRL, without first "meeting" them digitally, they often strike us as suspicious, like we can't imagine where they came from.

The lockdowns will only exacerbate this, forcing everyone into even less physical contact and more mutual suspicion ("social distancing" has of course been in effect for years now, but there's never been a better term for it). My generation's state of mind has to do with us, as millennials, having grown up not only in an age of ever-accelerating digital convenience, but also amidst the omnipresence of foreign wars that were (for most of us) never directly experienced. It was like living in a video game where we knew the stakes were real, yet could never perceive them as such. Same with mass shootings, which are intangible for all but a handful of us, and with the precarious nature of employment for almost all of us—every aspect of this has a video game quality, as we pilot our avatars through digital minefields, trying to earn dubiously fungible credit while avoiding landmines and pitfalls, and never being sure where, if anywhere, the rubber will meet the road.

Most young people today, at least in the so-called "rich world," have a vast breadth of digital experience but comparatively little IRL experience. Sex is just one facet of that, like a relic of how people used to be made. This is why the old polarities of liberal and conservative have grown so confusing—in the classic 60s sense of these terms, liberals were hippies who believed in free love and sex, while conservatives were squares who opposed those activities, but today many conservatives see themselves as actually "conserving" the sanctity of bodily contact, while liberals are accused of wanting to nullify it in favor of something far more mediated and abstract.

***The Opiate:** If you could give Gribby—and all those like him—one piece of advice about how not to go down the porn rabbit hole, what would it be?*

David Leo Rice: To have faith in something outside that matrix. For me in my moment of crisis, it was writing this story, and writing/art in general. I still, perhaps irrationally, or at least religiously, believe these processes are worthwhile. I believe they're redemptive in a way that nothing else is. I'm glad that I don't (yet) have to question this belief. It's an arbitrary but necessary determination of the "really real," outside all digital contingencies—a solid ground that I can plant my roots in. Maybe this is why fundamentalism of all kinds is growing around the world: people are desperate to put their faith in something, and there's no longer any way to derive that faith from the perceptible reality around

112

us, so it's being done more and more by fiat, which leads to ideological fanaticism and violence.

The drive to produce art serves as my anchor at the edge of the rabbit hole, keeping me at once from spiraling all the way down and from having to look away. Gribby, though he's not a bad person at heart, has no such anchor, and so, as a proxy for my own fears, he's the one whose fate is to take the plunge.

The Opiate: Do you feel that, in some sense, society was better off when it was forced to go into the trenches, so to speak, for its porn? — i.e. the "glory days" of 70s Times Square? In other words, does porn have more clout when it's not so "at one's disposal"?

David Leo Rice: Nostalgia interests me because I have such an ambivalent relation to it. On the one hand, yes, definitely. When I read about the seedy lifestyles of artists like Burroughs or Francis Bacon or Clive Barker, with all the drugs and prostitutes and orgies and disease and even death, or when I watch the films of John Waters or Fellini or Gus Van Sant, or read Samuel Delany and imagine going alone to a porn theater in Times Square in the 70s, it's hard not to romanticize that as the essence of the freedom we now lack—and much has been written about the dissolution of the "gay underground" after AIDS, and thereby the incorporation into mainstream commercial culture of one of the last truly alternative spaces in the postwar West.

Images of the Castro in San Francisco, or parts of New Orleans, or Paris, or the Japan of Shohei Imamura, or any famously seedy locales from bygone eras, are immediately romantic to me. There's an intrinsic fetish quality to anything forbidden, like the famed "back room" of the video store,

114

where kids of my generation knew the dirty movies were kept—and knew that everyone else knew as well, giving this private aspect of the individual a queasy but also humanizing public dimension. I'm glad that I have a "red light district of the mind" where I can go whenever I want, though part of me laments being unable to share it with other lechers and weirdos. Just as meditation and psychedelics have been coopted into life-hacks and self-care, this red light district now feels purged of any subversive potential.

At the same time, I'm skeptical of any "it was better then" kind of thinking. People always romanticize the past while being glad they don't live in it. If you asked me, right now, if we live in the worst of all possible worlds, I might glibly say yes, but if you then asked if I'd rather go back to a previous era, I'd say no.

The Opiate: Is this one of the more taboo/lurid subjects you've addressed in your work? And does it come from a more personal place than some of your other pieces?

David Leo Rice: I'm always trying to push boundaries in ways that feel productive, to "get under the hood" by making people just uncomfortable enough to engage with a different perspective on reality. This book is my most sustained onslaught of X-rated material, though it's also my most overtly mystical. The medieval mysticism I studied in college posited a sexual relation between the individual and the cosmos—each endlessly penetrating and generating the other, which often resulted in extreme pleas, on the part of the mystic, to fuck or be fucked by God— so this was my attempt to update that style of writing for our digital age, and to posit a persistence of human yearning for

116

the beyond even as technology warps and expands (or shrinks) our notion of what and where that might be.

This book was more personal in that it came from a reaction of visceral disgust at myself for bingeing on so much data while also fixating on my own impotence in the face of what seemed like a global catastrophe, or age of catastrophes, though it was also less personal in that most of my work takes place in towns like the one I grew up in, whereas this one takes place in a generic megacity, with a generic everyman at its center, and partakes of the media theory I read later in life.

2022 addendum questions

The Opiate: What's your current take on the continued oracular quality of this novella? Did you ever imagine, in your most depraved vision (i.e., this), how much "the Gribby life" would come to fruition as a result of our prolonged (non-)existence in lockdown, trapped inside with nothing but the screen as our "savior"?

David Leo Rice: It's shocking how quickly the most "out there" parts of this book came to pass during the two years between its first and second editions. I put a lot of faith in the idea that "the story is smarter than you are," in the sense that fiction can serve as an oracular practice if you allow it to. If you start writing from a vague hunch or feeling about the world, without trying too hard to spell it out (as you would have to in a piece of nonfiction), often you'll find that truths you weren't consciously aware of will crystallize and hatch when you go back and read what you wrote. As humans we have so many sensing systems that are deeper, or at least quicker, than conscious knowledge, so if you write in a semi-unconscious manner—hypnotizing yourself by focusing on the immediate story, rather than any underlying themes or ideas—you often end up giving voice to things that you "don't know you know" (to bastardize Donald Rumsfeld's infamous phrase).

The Opiate: Did you "not know you knew" about just how predatory the internet might become? Particularly with no other way to scam and prey on people in the absence of being able to do so tangibly while everyone was in lockdown mode?

David Leo Rice: Looking back on this book with the hindsight of the Covid lockdowns, the George Floyd protests, January 6th, the war in Ukraine, and the explosion of conspiracy thinking around all these events, to say nothing of the apparent rise of the Metaverse and the deeply strange doings in the finance/crypto world, I can see how the writing process, completed between 2017 and 2019, began to articulate the feeling, which is much clearer now, of how humans have entered into a mutually predatory relationship with the outside world: on the one hand, during the lockdowns, many of us avoided the outside world altogether, for fear that it wanted to prey on us, while also coming more and more to prey on it by proxy, plugging into the internet to a truly unprecedented degree in a desperate desire to feed on the same external world that we were so afraid would feed on us.

The Opiate: Speaking of being "fed on," do you notice elements of the post-Trump political scene infiltrating your prose? And what predictions do you have about the future, as far as politics go? Full-tilt dystopia or...?

David Leo Rice: I've always been interested in times and places where the imminent and the transcendent come together, so lately I've been drawn to the feeling of terrestrial politics turning into something nearly extraterrestrial, where the realm of human argument takes on the quality of an apocalyptic battle between angels and demons, or humanity and its antithesis. I think the whole 2020s will be riven by these battles, as humanity keeps struggling to persist against the encroachment and interpenetration of algorithmic and robotic technologies, as well as the increasingly complex processes that seem to freight elections with sky-high stakes while also perhaps nullifying any possible outcome, insofar as the "people" elected, whoever they may be, will be less and less in charge. Whether or not this account of the current and coming moment will prove to be "true," I think it will become increasingly irresistible.

The Opiate: More than anywhere else in the world, the U.S. was the country that displayed the most resistance to wearing masks throughout the pandemic, making it a kind of "political statement" somehow. How do you feel this relates to the overarching theme of your novella vis-à-vis mind vs. body/body vs. mind?

David Leo Rice: Watching the cultural polarization in the U.S. around Covid policy unfold, where one segment of the population wanted total lockdowns and one wanted none at all, I did think about the relation of the mind to the body. One side seemed to be saying, "We want to think and talk about Covid all the time, filling our minds with it so as to spare our bodies," while the other side said, "We want to risk our bodies so as to keep our minds free from having to think or talk about it at all."

On some level, both adaptations make sense—each is sacrificing one system for the sake of the other in a poignant devil's bargain. This looped back to Gribby's conundrum with porn, and by extension his conundrum with his entire bodily existence, or lack thereof: is he sacrificing his body to satisfy the cravings of his mind, or sacrificing his mind to satisfy the cravings of his body?

The Opiate: With the body seemingly constantly on the brain at this moment in time, it seems timely that the body horror genre has undeniably returned to cinema in a big way since The PornME Trinity's *initial release. This includes the Ballard-esque* Titane *and Cronenberg's* Crimes of the Future. *Do you feel the decay/sickness of the body becoming such a topic again is a subconscious response to the pandemic?*

David Leo Rice: Absolutely. One major project of mine over the past two years has been co-editing (with the Scottish author Chris Kelso) an anthology about Cronenberg's work, entitled *Children of the New Flesh.* Chris and I immersed ourselves in revisiting Cronenberg and the body horror boom of the 80s, as well as considering his new film and *Titane,* and really thinking about why this approach feels so relevant and vital today.

As part of this project, I started thinking about "portal phases" in history, and how they appear in pop culture. The 80s was one portal phase (through which Chris and I emerged into the world), toward the end of the Cold War and the rise of the internet. Many films from that time featured literal portals, whether of the domestic variety, like the TV set in *Poltergeist*, or the extraterrestrial variety, as in any number of alien and UFO movies, and now we're on the cusp of another portal phase.

The Opiate: *What would you predict is on the other side of that cusp?*

David Leo Rice: It's hard to say, but it feels like the end of the "screen age," which has dominated the twenty-first century so far, and the beginning of an age of total immersion, where there will be no difference at all between being online and offline. The ubiquity of smartphones means this is already pretty much the case, but it feels like soon the virtual environment will be even more immersive and the question of what the body is, and what it's for, will become even more painful—which is part of why body horror has made a resurgence. It was also telling to work on this book against the backdrop of the Covid vaccines, and to imbibe both the triumphalism, from one side, and the abject horror, from the other, about the scientific evolution they represent, and what that might mean for human bodies going forward—is it a step toward immortality or a step toward obsolescence?

The whole pandemic is ambiguous in this regard, since, on the one hand, it re-embodied everyone, making us newly aware of the fragility of our physical health and the interconnectedness of the physical communities we either retreated into or kept away from, and yet, on the other hand, it also sundered the last physical connections we had to one another, rendering almost all activities into virtual ghosts of their former selves.

The Opiate: *One activity, at least, that hasn't suffered from the virtual reckoning is the prolificness of your writing. What projects have you released since* The PornME Trinity *and to what extent have they held up to your previous commitment to "making art from reality, rather than trying to mirror or 'keep up with' reality, a project whose futility (both in the sense of being impossible, and of being pointless, even if possible) should now be clear to everyone"?*

David Leo Rice: I've released two novels—*A Room in Dodge City, Vol. 2,* the middle link in a trilogy that should be completed in 2023, and *The New House,* a standalone novel about a family of Jewish outsider artists, loosely inspired by the worlds of Joseph Cornell—as well as a story collection, *Drifter,* that gathers most of my stories from 2010-2020, and the Cronenberg book mentioned before.

In that book, I defined the archetypal Cronenberg character, seen in *Videodrome, The Fly* and *Dead Ringers*, as the "heroic pervert," a character who becomes heroic not by venturing out to slay the dragon and save the village, but by willingly and knowingly succumbing to the sickness and depravity of a given moment, in order to overcome denial and face reality head-on. By the end of *The PornME Trinity*, Gribby becomes a junior version of the heroic pervert—he doesn't save anyone, least of all himself, but he does transform from a hapless subjugated pawn to someone who sees the machinery of subjugation for what it is, and thus attains a semi-divine power over his own fate, even if he can't alter it.

I try to apply this principle to my own production and, hopefully, I've succeeded to some degree in these new projects. Going back to an idea mentioned earlier, I try to access as much of what I "don't know I know" as I can, hoping to "catch" the strands passing through the ether in a given moment, and relate them to something deeper and more lasting than the endless, sickening churn of the media feed—something that this feed touches on and activates within us, but that is never visible on its surface. In short, though I'm glad to have survived this era so far, I don't want to avoid its sickness. I want to catch it in a way I can harness rather than succumb to, or harness by succumbing to.

ACKNOWLEDGEMENTS

I am sincerely grateful to the following people, for their incisive and sustained help on this project: Genna Rivieccio, for her ongoing editorial vision and support, over the years, and for making this book a reality; Laura Mega for her indelible cover artwork; John Kazanjian, Michael Natalie, Eli Epstein-Deutsch, Andrei Cristea and Rob Rice for their feedback at numerous points along the way; Nicholas Watson and Steven Rozenski for their tutelage in the mystical fringes of the middle ages; Lynn and Richard Rice for raising me to both love books and see the innate strangeness of reality; and to Ingrid Gustafson, for her unconditional love, belief and support, and her insight into the unchanging essence of human nature. It'd be just Gribby in space without all of you.

David Leo Rice is the author of the novels *Angel House*, *The New House*, and the *Dodge City* trilogy, and co-editor of *Children of the New Flesh: The Early Work and Pervasive Influence of David Cronenberg*. Rice's story collection, *Drifter*, was named one of the best books of 2021 in the *Southwest Review* and *Locus Magazine*, and his next collection, *The Squimbop Condition*, will be out in 2023. Keep up-to-date with his work at www.raviddice.com.

Photo by: Ellen Augarten